My Resilience Workbook

2ⁿᵈ edition

Naomi L. Baum, Ph.D.

with Batya Rotter and Estie Reidler

My Resilience Workbook – Second Edition
Introduction for Teachers and Parents:

Children exposed to natural disasters, threat of terrorist attacks, illness, and other traumas, may feel anxious, vulnerable and can develop a variety of symptoms ranging from clinginess to difficulties sleeping. While the great majority of children show natural resilience and do not go on to develop post traumatic stress disorder (PTSD), adults can help children strengthen their natural resilience and coping mechanisms. This workbook was developed to help do just that.

"My Resilience Workbook", 2nd edition, will provide children an opportunity to express the wide range of feelings they are experiencing, while also allowing them to become more comfortable talking about some of their more difficult ones. Understanding and communicating about feelings is at the root of resilience. We hope that you will use this workbook as a catalyst for conversation about stressful topics, feelings, or difficult issues with your child or in the classroom. The workbook can be used at home, daycare or school settings in both group or individual format. It can be used in clinical or therapeutic settings as well. The younger the child the more he or she will need adult guidance when working in the workbook. An older child will be able to work independently. You are encouraged to talk with your children about what they have drawn and written.

The workbook, in addition to developing a vocabulary for emotions, encourages a sense of safety, coping skills, social supports and hope, all of which have been identified as important in building and maintaining personal resilience. They form the cornerstones of the "Building Resilience Intervention" (BRI) a workshop series that was developed along with the original workbook at Metiv-The Israel Center for the Treatment of Psychotrauma, Jerusalem.

The first edition of this workbook has been used very effectively in pre-school settings in Israel where children were exposed to ongoing rocket attacks and war, in Haiti, Nepal and Chili after earthquake, in New York City after Hurricane Sandy, and more. The workbook has been translated to Hebrew, Arabic, Spanish, French and Amharic. We welcome future translations.

We wish you much luck in using this workbook and would be very happy to receive your feedback and suggestions.

For more information on Building Resilience Intervention (BRI) and for feedback please contact:
Dr, Naomi Baum
Naomi.baum@gmail.com
www.naomibaum.com

A percentage of the proceeds from the sale of this workbook will be donated to Metiv-ICTP for their work with children suffering from trauma.

My name: _____

My age: _____

My school: _____

My grade:_____

Something interesting about me:_____

_____

This is a picture of me….

This is a picture of my family.

When I feel happy...

When I feel happy or excited, this is how I show it:

_____

_____

Things that make me feel happy:

_____

_____

_____

When I feel happy or excited, my body feels...

_____

_____

_____

When I feel happy or excited, I like to:

_____

_____

_____

When I feel sad....

People can tell when I am sad because I:
_____
_____
_____

Things that make me feel sad:
_____
_____
_____

When I am sad this is what happens in my body:
_____
_____

When I am sad I like to:
_____
_____
_____

When I feel scared...

When I feel scared,
my body feels:

_____

_____

Things that make me feel scared:

_____

_____

Things that help me when
I feel scared:

_____

_____

When I feel scared, I
like to:

_____

_____

_____

When I feel angry...

Things that make me feel angry:

_____
_____
_____

Things that help me when I am angry:

_____
_____
_____

When I feel angry this is what happens in my body:

_____
_____
_____

When I feel angry, this is how I show it:

_____
_____
_____

Connect a line from the feeling to the matching face

angry

worried

funny

tired

sad

How do I feel today?

happy

afraid

excited

When I feel...

Choose an emotion for each box and then fill in your answers

When I feel _____
I always _____
_____

When I feel _____
_____

I never _____
_____
_____

When I feel _____
_____

I sometimes ____
_____

When I feel _____
I like to _____
_____

Draw a line to show where you feel this feeling in your body?

SAD

HAPPY

WORRIED

ANGRY

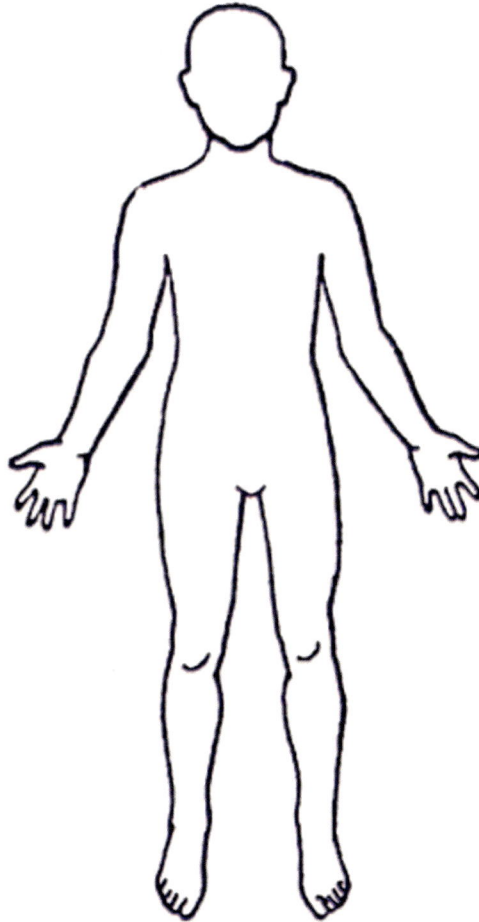

LOVE

SCARED

What helps me calm down?

Draw a circle around the things that help you:

SPEAKING WITH MY MOM OR DAD

MUSIC

PLAYING WITH FRIENDS

READING BOOKS

What else helps you calm down? Draw it.

How lovely!

Something nice happened to me today:

_____
_____
_____
_____
_____
_____
_____

Something not so nice happened to me today:

_____
_____
_____
_____
_____
_____
_____

Ouch, the thorns!

What helps me to feel safe and strong...

FRIENDS

FAMILY

HOPE

LOVE

Draw a special place where you feel happy and safe

What are you grateful for?

I am thankful for:

1 _____
2 _____
3 _____

Who and what help you when you are feeling bad? Draw your answers in the circles.

Talking to friends helps me

Going for a walk helps me

"Hope is a thing with feathers..." E. Dickinson

What are you hopeful for?

Draw what your hope looks like.

How do you feel today?

Circle how you feel each day. Use as many faces as you want.

Sunday	Monday	Tuesday	Wednesday	Thursday	Friday	Saturday

Made in the USA
Las Vegas, NV
07 February 2025